WAR

A Letter From Peace

WAR

A Letter From Peace

Written By Dwayne A. Cannon

Publisher: Emerge Productions Group LLC.

Cover Illustration By Juan Osborne

WAR

A Letter From Peace

Salute to everybody who's dying to get away

*From someone else's physical **War***

And everybody who's living

*To gain some of their own mental **Peace**.*

WAR

A Letter From Peace

*Try not to run around with **War** today*

*When you're out and about **In The World**-*

Because** it might just be the reason **Peace

***Walked Away** from you yesterday.*

WAR

A Letter From Peace

A Short Story Between War & Peace Explained...

"War is a state or a nation that's in conflict, that's armed between the two groups. War is also considered a competition, generated from the hostility of the people, who's condition was particularly unpleasant. War is an engagement, that's carried out by a force to be reckoned with"

"Peace is the peacemaker, the period in which there is no War, or the War has ended. Peace is Freedom from disturbance and tranquility, it is righteousness, justice and prosperity. Peace gives a person a piece of mind spiritually, it's the opposite of one being stressed, anxious or the feeling of one being unease"

WAR

A Letter From Peace

*Let me take you on an historic and epic adventure about **War** and his lifelong enemy **Peace** who helped War, in restoring some Peace one day on the block of confusion, between trouble street and problem ave. It was a militant day and War was outside on general purpose, War decided to march around the corner where he saw Peace standing there peacefully. So, out of jealousy, envy and hate War intentionally bumped into Peace in order to get him upset and angry.*

And with all due respect, Peace humbly turned around with no hesitation, opened his arms and extended out his hands hoping to embrace War with nothing but love. War was not impressed by the act and had all intentions on starting a war, instead War looked at Peace up and down before frowning his face and with no respect, he slowly walked around Peace while roughly rubbing his shoulder up against his.

*War was always surprised and could never understand, how Peace continued to acknowledge him whenever they bumped into each other on the block of confusion, between trouble street and problem ave. Even after all the harmful and injurious situations War had caused, since War was just a struggle and Peace was still striving to gain a little bit of **Freedom**.*

As kids War and Peace played on the block of confusion, between trouble street and problem ave. Where they both witnessed a whole lot of shootings, killings, rapes, domestic violence, racism, police brutality, drug abuse, suicide and just about everything a child or any dignity decision making adult, shouldn't be subjected to when outside in this world.

Growing up this was everything that forced Peace to want to end War and War wanting to end Peace. But if you was to asked War how he felt about Peace, he would tell you his duties in this world was not to adapt peacefully, but to make sure when people go into battles they choose to go to War.

*Because everybody knows once you win the battle, you've just about won the entire War. And if you asked Peace how he felt about War, he would tell you that War has always been a big struggle and throughout those struggles, War always had to fight in order to get close to Peace. And that's why when Peace was around War, Peace never choose sides Peace just strived for a little bit of Freedom and always choose a piece of mind. Since kids War and Peace has always been rivals, they both stayed involved in every hostile and injustice encounter anyone has ever seen or encountered in the world. And most of their fall outs often have escalated by a gang of bullies and troublemakers, who calls themselves **Violence**.*

*Violence was someone Peace wish was dead, and War wish he could just kill already. Being that Violence has always been the main cause to why War and Peace had to meet. Violence was also the cause to why so many lives have been lost, why so many individuals were incarcerated and on death row, why domestic violence ruined good relationships, why children never got to see their 4th birthday, why police brutality ended in death, why drug wars continue, why guns were being sold in every community, why bombers committed suicide, Why religions are hated and why **Racism** rubbed shoulders and ran with **Beef** for 400 plus years. Violence also hangs on the block of confusion between trouble street and problem ave, where everybody fears him. Only because Violence shakes hands with all the weapons and gives out injuries to the innocent while assaulting whoever runs with Peace. And whenever his comrade Beef shows his face on the block, grudges and conflicts starts to escalate, while Beef stands there arguing with himself calling out to Violence by his first name.*

*Racism used to live on the block of confusion, between trouble street and problem ave until he moved, due to War and Peace becoming friends. Racism was tough, he was a bully who pushed Peace to wanting to become friends with Violence. Racism had always been distance friends with Violence and whenever Violence occurred, Racism was always around but never would show his face. Unless there were two different races involved, or unless his family members **Jealousy**, **Envy** and **Hate** was standing there next to Violence.*

Especially if what they were doing was always better, Jealousy had lived with nothing but resentment and wanted his brothers Envy and Hate to help him put an end to Peace, by taking away his Freedom, with the help of Racisms friend Beef.

Envy was the second oldest of the three, his resentment was aroused by someone else's possessions and what he couldn't have. Envy would do whatever Jealousy would say, which not only manipulated Hate, but it also made Hate dislike everybody who stood for Peace or stood next to Peace. Hate was the youngest of the three brothers and walked around with a heart that was stone cold, being that Hate was born prejudice. Now standing in the middle of trouble street on the corner of confusion, between problem ave, War and Peace are talking to each other about their next move and how they plan to fight Violence back and bring Peace back to the block. But first they had to find a way to kill Racisms family members Jealousy, Envy and Hate.

Peace: Well if it isn't my lifelong childhood friend and brother War. I see you still have unresolved political, domestic and race issues going in the world and on trouble street, on the corner of confusion between problem ave.

War: And if it isn't my stop the violence, all lives matter, peace in the middle east childhood friend. Who wants the whole world to get along, by carrying some Peace with them. But what he doesn't realize is that without War, there wouldn't be no Peace.

Peace: So, War How's all those useless battles your always in the middle of, where not only innocent people die but they die at the hands of other innocent people. Who are forced to go to War, just because some people who are in position of power, still don't realize that the power in their position is temporary.

War: To be honest Peace, there's really nothing I can do about that. I never supported people dying, I'm only involved because some people can't get along and most people believe that this world and land belongs to them. So, when the Beef they are in causes Violence I'm called upon and I respect battles.

Peace: As much as I dislike saying this, but you definitely have a point War and speaking of respect, I have a letter I want you to read concerning what you just said.

"Jealousy, Envy and Hate were three brothers who indulged in nothing but evil acts, they were also related to Racism, with Jealousy being the oldest who always was the first to get that feeling of insecurity, fear and concern of what someone else had, or what someone else was doing"

War looks down at the waist of Peace and notices an envelope in his right hand. War lifts his head back up and looks Peace directly in his eyes. Before turning his head to the his left and looking up and down trouble street, on the corner of confusion, between problem ave. For any signs of Beef and Violence. Peace raises his right arm while starring War directly back in his face, Peace extends out his arm with the envelope loosely held in his hand. Peace, then lightly taps War in the chest with the envelope, War looks at the envelope after looking back at Peace.

Peace: War what's your opinion on the "All Lives Matter" Movement and what do you think should be done about all the unarmed innocent people, getting shot and killed by the police.

War looks at Peace like if this should be a question, he might want to ask Racism or Violence. They both get quiet, War then puts his head down for a quick moment and shakes his head, War lifts his head back up and just before he answers the question. Peace grabs War's right arm and places the envelope in his hand.

Peace: By the way, after you finish reading the letter, I would highly appreciate it if you would share this letter with **Revenge**, **Penalty** and **Vengeance.** The letter concerns some serious and personal matters in the world, that involves these three back stabbers we both knew, since you were struggling in racist battles, and I was running with slaves looking for Freedom.

War: Are you talking about Jealousy, Envy and Hate who lives on trouble street near the corner of confusion, between problem ave.

Peace: Yes, and since Revenge, Penalty and Vengeance have been trying to end them since Jealousy was just a snotty nose feeling and Envy was a dirty pamper running around possessive and Hate was a little brat who realized he disliked everything better than him. I know they won't have a problem with helping us both, get rid of all of them and start restoring some worldwide Peace.

"Revenge was like the enforcer in the family, he was the one who enforced harm, injury and pain to anyone who went around wrongly causing innocent people to suffer, Revenge loved to retaliate and punish those who was done wrong"

"Penalty had more of a jurisdiction mentality, he took people to court on the street and if you were convicted, you were sent to see one of his brothers, either Vengeance or Revenge. Penalty treated broken codes in the street, the same as broken contracts or spoken agreements that ended up getting their honest oath broke"

"Vengeance helped out Revenge carry out the punishment and inflicted pain and injury to those that were doing wrong. Vengeance, dealt with feelings surrounded around anger, he was bad and the meanest of the three and didn't like no one, Vengeance nickname was payback. But what confused people is when they weren't all together, they always got mistaken for one another being that they were triplet twins"

While standing there, War opens the envelope unfolds the paper and starts reading what's written inside the letter inside, War then folds the letter back up after he finish reading it. Places the letter in his pocket and walks away from Peace. War looks at Peace again before taking a few steps back, now a few inches away from Peace, with a look of confusion like he was surprised that Peace had even given him something. Only due to the fact that since they were adults, War and Peace had been in more violent wars, than there were presidents elected in the united States.

War: No problem Peace and you know what, let me stand right here and read it in front of you so I can get more familiar with what you are up to and what's going on and while I'm reading it, keep a look out for your boy Violence you know how you, him, and his gang get down. They should be on their way here now, being that with all these people out here watching me and you standing here talking to one another, which is not what they are used to.

Peace: Violence War, really! You got jokes! But you don't have to tell me twice, Violence and me never did get along, I try and stay away from people like that and I stay away far away from Jealousy, Envy and Hate as well.

War: Peace, Only because I don't want any life changing, unnecessary confrontations and altercation popping off, that might lead to me getting involved and having a War with you.

Peace: I understand War! And we all know if me and you get involved in a Violent War, it's going to take more than a few freedom fighters to help calm things down.

War: Your absolutely right Peace! Then it might take years or even decades before any of the madness comes to an end, if it decides to come to an end because we both know that Religious, Government, Civil, Revolutionary, Political, Military, Race etc. all have one thing in common when it comes down to Violent Wars.

Peace: And what might that be, a Peaceful War?

War: Death! You see Peace, in my Wars people lose and when they have to personally deal with Violence, they lose their life. And remember it's hard to reconcile when in a War, especially when the world only settle things by way of Pain and Harm, which will definitely end in a whole lot of bloodshed.

The Letter...

To: Revenge, Penalty and Vengeance

This is Peace, you all should remember me from whenever me and War had Beef that always escalated from small disagreements, then turned into physical altercations, that most of the time ended In painful Violence. I just wanted to reach out to you all on a few issues at hand, concerning a few people you despise and are definitely familiar with. This comes as no surprise plus I am trying to avoid getting War involved in another War, that has been causing me some problems since and before "The First War" better known as "The Seminal Catastrophe" dated back in 1914. These backstabbing snakes continue and won't stop initiating trouble and being the core of 100% of these problems in the world. Revenge, Penalty and Vengeance you all know I am all about Peace, but Jealousy, Envy and Hate has to go, and they all are way overdue. You all should be familiar with **Discipline** *and* **Justice** *from uptown, they have been in battles and combats with me and War ever since I can remember. Revenge, Penalty and Vengeance my life and heart won't allow me to handle these guys like I know you all could, and I've made up in my mind to let you all handle the situation. It's seems like Jealousy walks around with grudges of Envy on each of his shoulders, with a stomach filled with undeniable backstabbing Hate.*

Jealousy, Envy and Hate seems to be all around us, in our homes, at our place of work, at our children schools, outside of people's relationships, In the world and definitely in people's hearts. Again Revenge, Penalty and Vengeance Myself and War need your help unconditional, the world needs your help, and this is exactly why I wrote this letter. Not only to get some Justice, but to get Revenge on Jealousy, to make Envy worry and to cause Hate to start disliking himself.

P.S.
I will also be contacting and meeting up with Freedom, who will accompany me when it's time to see Revenge, Penalty and Vengeance.

Your Solider and Comrade Peace!

"Discipline and Justice" live and die to uphold Peace regardless of who is involved or who initiated it and who they think might be part of the problem. Discipline trains people's behavior using aggressive punishment, Disciplines duties on this earth is to correct disrespectful disobedience. While discipline Justice initiates is all about fairness and being reasonable. Justice lays the law down like a courtroom, the only difference is Justice isn't always controlled by the law"

WAR

A Letter From Peace

Jealousy, Envy and Hate was always trying to get War and Violence to hang out with this kid from across town name **Harm,** *who since an injury playing in the sandbox, always looked up to War and Violence.*

Harm always thought that if he could get acknowledged by War and liked by Violence he could and would go around causing Harm to anyone and everyone who disrespected Him, for taking his kindness for weakness.

"Harm dealt with the physical or mental damage of a person; he also was the

appointment to the Pain of someone feeling hurt"

Down the block on trouble street near the corner of confusion, between problem ave, was **Pain** *who was related to Harm through marriage. Pain only showed his face either when Harm was involved, or he had heard that Violence had a physical altercation.*

"Pain was the epidemy of what Violence and War stood for, Pain embodied

them, he would eat, sleep and drink what Violence and War became when in

battles standing together"

***B**ut War was cut from a different cloth, he was raised by both of his parents **Civil** and **Revolution**, who warned and raised War since a kid to stay as far away from all of them as he could. Especially Violence, because Revolution knew Violence was good at instigating problems that influenced and tricked the weak into going to War and Civil knew that Violence loved when her son War would get involved.*

***P**eace really did hate Violence, Jealousy, Envy, Hate, Pain and Harm with a passion, and they all knew it, so Peace decided to give them all a nick name and whenever Peace would run into one of them, he would call them by their nick name. Violence was **Path To Destruction**...*
*Jealousy was **No Self Confidence**...Envy was **Lil Jealousy**...Hate was **Hostile Disgust**...Pain was **Ill Injury**...and Harm was called **Ill Suffering***

"*Civil was a fan of ordinary citizens, she always would listen to their concerns and problems. She was raised to be courteous and polite but when a war in the country between citizens arrived, Civil would have to call on her husband Revolution. Now Revolution was militant he was a force to be reckoned with, when it was time to overthrow, Revolution's present would change society and the social structure that was accompanied by War and Violence*"

WAR

A Letter From Peace

*You could **Give Any Child** on earth **A Gun***

***And Eventually**, they will grow up raising bullets-*

But if you give a bullet, to any gun on earth

*Eventually, a lot of **Children Won't** be fortunate enough to **Grow Up**.*

WAR

A Letter From Peace

War and Peace separate from each other, as War starts walking to where Revenge, Penalty and Vengeance are so, they can read the letter. Peace walks around the corner and down the block where he spots Beef standing there on the corner talking to Pain and Harm, they all see Peace walking towards them. So, Pain and Harm leaves the scene while Beef stands there and greets Peace with a head nod as he approaches, Peace greets him back with a head nod signaling hello back., Peace stands in front of Beef and shakes his head side to side, signaling that he doesn't agree with Beef talking to Pain and Harm.

Beef: We'll if it isn't the infamous Peace, the worlds mental serenity, the calm before the storm, the righteous prosperity for all mankind. I don't know but I had this feeling you would be here. I was supposed to meeting someone here, they had something for me. None of your business though.

Peace: You don't say, we'll you are the bad seed Beef, who I just saw talking to two of my enemies again, what are trying to start a War, or didn't you get the memo.

Beef: I should be asking you that question, being that this is me and Violence block. You are the one trespassing, do you know where you are and I heard you and War was talking around the corner, on my block of confusion, between trouble street and problem ave so, what's that all about Peace, what are you passing out some Freedom.

Peace: Of course we were talking, you know exactly what I'm about and after all, I stopped a lot of people around these parts from getting shot and killed, a lot of seniors citizens from getting robbed, a lot of kids from getting bullied, a lot of woman from getting raped, a lot of businesses from getting robbed and I ceased a whole lot of rival, civil and domestic Wars. So, with no due respect Mr. Beef, I believe I have more right to be here than you will ever have.

Beef looks up and down the block in confusion, troubling he shakes his head side to side, signaling that he strongly disagrees with what Peace just said. Beef sucks his teeth, raises his middle finger and frowns with an expression of confusion all over his face.

Which only reminded Peace that the expressions on Beef's face, could only mean one thing, Peace had hit a nerve and the last time Beef felt that way, people saw him talking to Violence, Pain and Harm and the rest is history. Once War ran into Revenge, Penalty and Vengeance War wasted no time handing the letter he got from Peace over to them, Revenge opens the letter, looks at it and starts reading outload. After Revenge finish reading the letter, Revenge turns around in the direction of Penalty and Vengeance. Revenge tells them to get ready, because it's time to go with War and find Peace. War interrupts Revenge and explains to all of them that, before they can go and find Peace, they should first recruit Discipline and Justice, to help in the planning of getting murderous Revenge on Jealousy, while Envy is getting hit with a deadly Penalty, right before they all inflict the wrath of Vengeance down on Hate.

War, Revenge, Penalty and Vengeance all leave the block of confusion between trouble street and problem ave, to go and find Discipline and Justice. They walk down the block as they all approach the corner Penalty spots Peace standing there talking to Beef. War questions them about why Beef is Beef waving his hands in the air, like he's ready to swing on Peace so, they all stop and watch from a distance. They watch Peace as he stands there and listens so, War, Revenge, Penalty and Vengeance, all walk up and stand behind Peace, Revenge taps Peace on his right shoulder Peace turns to his right and see's War, Revenge Penalty and Vengeance standing there with the same look on all of their faces. The look is so furious Peace even had to take a second look at them all, just to make sure the look they had wasn't targeted towards him.

War steps in-between Revenge and Peace, he stands directly in front on Beef, while Penalty and Vengeance grabs Peace by the arm and pulls him back behind War to stand with them. Beef is petrified, he looks at War with fear in his eyes, Beef then looks at Peace and sweat starts developing above and around his forehead. Then all a sudden turning the corner, slowly walking up behind Beef is Discipline and Justice.

They are furious, in rage and full of anger so, Beef tries to take a sidestep away from them all, in order to get out of the fearful and frightening situation he has been put in. Beef holds his head down, until he hears his name being called from across the street, Beef lifts his head quickly back up and to his surprise, there walking down the block on the other side of the street, was Jealousy, Envy and Hate.

But the strangest thing to Beef was the look on their faces, Jealousy looked like he was so confused, Envy looked like he was in trouble and Hate looked like he was dealing with some major problems. As they all walked into the middle of the street, War and Peace looks at Jealousy, Discipline and Justice looks at Envy while Revenge, Penalty and Vengeance is starring at Hate. Now Beef realize, that everyone has their attention on someone, so now would be a good time to make his escape from the circle of heated interrogation, that really felt like the fire pit of hell. So, Beef slowly moves to the side and quickly start walking in the direction, where Jealousy, Envy and Hate are now standing in the middle of the street, on the block of confusion between trouble street and problem ave.

War, Revenge, Penalty, Vengeance, Discipline and Justice all start walking towards the middle of the street, while Peace stands on the sidewalk and watches from the sideline. Peace wanted to kill Jealousy, Envy and Hate a minute ago but when he thought about, what really might happen Peace started getting second thoughts. Peace was now thinking of different ways and options to settle what could end in pure bloodshed and all he could think about, was that somebodies' blood would be on his hand. This was definitely something Peace didn't want or need, being that Peace stood for freedom, Peace was mental serenity, Peace was a state or period where there was no fights or War, Peace was the one who could bring together harmony, between groups, nations, worlds and rivals. And this was definitely the opposite, of what Peace stood for.

As people drove down the block and some looking out their windows, pedestrians walking through the block all watch trying to figure out, what all the commotion was about. Some locked their car doors while others let down their blinds, a few pedestrians crossed on the other side of the street. Hoping to avoid whatever was about to happen here on the block of confusion, between trouble street and problem ave.

With the tension and energy boiling in the middle of the street, there were some nosey adults and teenagers strangling by who decided to stop and be nosey. And in no time, there was a lot of bad energy surrounding the entire area, followed by heavy hostility, ugly animosity and a whole lot of bitter resentment. Peace steps off the sidewalk and walks out into the middle of the street, a few feet away from everyone else, he walks around War and Vengeance and right up to Jealousy, Envy and Hate while looking back and forth at Beef, through the corner of his eyes. Peace reaches into his back pocket and begins to pull something out, until he hears Wars voice yelling at him from a few feet away in the middle of the street.

Now yelling at the top of his lungs, War tries his best to stop Peace from reaching into his pocket, as he slowly walk towards Beef, Jealousy, Envy and Hate. While everybody from teenagers to senior citizens in their home, looking out their windows to cars driving by slowly with their windows down. To the strangling pedestrians who's still standing feet away, all hoping to see and find out what's happening on the block of confusion, between trouble street and problem ave.

Peace pays attention to the voice, so he decides to turn around and look in the direction where the voice is coming from, Peace takes a step back, removes his hand from his back pocket and notices a shadow turning the corner, reflecting from under the streetlight. The shadow gets bigger and the light follows the shadow into the street. Peace looks at War before he starts walking in the direction towards the voice and the shadow. Peace then stops in his tracks and realizes that the voice and the shadow under the light, was his long los comrade **Freedom.**

"Freedom gave Peace the power and the right to speak freely, the power to think

positive without hindrance, whenever situations like this arrived. Peace always

felt like when Freedom was around, there was no one being mentally or

physically imprisoned, or anyone worried about being enslaved, from not

having the ability to change and this was exactly what Peace was on this earth

for, Freedom"

While Freedom and Peace stand by the curb next to the sidewalk, Peace suddenly starts to hear massive commotion, yelling and loud voices screaming from behind him, so he quickly turns around and see's War, Revenge, Penalty, Vengeance, Discipline and Justice all surrounding Jealousy, Envy, Hate and Beef. Not saying a word, Beef quietly and secretively moves further and further away from the group, now standing across the street far away from where the tension has erupted. Beef stands there and tries to blend in with the straggling pedestrians, adults and teenagers standing next to him, as he watches everybody who's involved in the dispute in the street, creating havoc and chaos.

Peace looks at War, War looks back at Peace and then they both turn and look at the mob of furious, angry and hot tempered "Lives Matter" individuals walking up the block in the middle of the street towards them.

Peace notices that not one person is smiling, or even has a look regarding that they are being amused, by the situation occurring in front of them, on the block of confusion, between trouble street and problem ave. As the block fills with a mob of non-segregated individuals, all wearing black t-shirts some with "Lives Matter" written on the front. They are all standing side by side, shoulder to shoulder, with their arms interlocked different races and creeds from African Americans, Caucasian, Chinese, Indian, Hispanic etc. They all are standing there color blind, to the preconceived options of the world, that a lot of people feel is based on physical characteristics and social qualities, as they embrace sending a message of unity.

***"Lives Matter" follows in the shadow of the "Black Lives Matter" movement
and is a gratifying response to how the movement, supports African American
political activism in communities, that campaigns against violence and racism
towards all black human beings. "Black Lives Matter" also emphasizes their
rights about racial equality, economic justice and political power. A political
intervention, in a world where Black lives are systematically and intentionally
targeted for demise. It is an affirmation of black people's contributions to this
society and humanity, and their resilience in the face of deadly oppression.***

*While the "Lives Matter" mob of individuals flood the streets on the block of
confusion, between trouble street and problem ave militant, shoulder to shoulder.
Peace and Freedom make their way over to where Beef is standing, still trying to
blend in with the crowd of pedestrians across the street. War watches Peace and
Freedom while Vengeance, Penalty, Revenge, Discipline and Justice all watch
Jealousy, Envy and Hate just to make sure neither of them try and make a sudden
move on Peace or Freedom. Once Peace and Freedom are across the street,
Freedom stands there looking for Beef, while Peace looks at the mob of
individuals standing there, side by side shoulder to shoulder, with their arms
interlocked militantly.*

*Peace realizes that the mob is here for a real reason, a reason that should be
making statement, not just to the streets but to the world. Then it dawned on
Peace, that the mob of individuals had Freedom and they knew Freedom is what
gave "Lives Matter" the power and the right to speak, walk and act freely,
Freedom is what gave them the power to think positive without hindrance,
whenever situations like this arrived. Freedom showed the "Lives Matter" mob of
individuals that with Freedom, there was no being mentally or physically
imprisoned and anyone that was worried about being enslaved, from not having
the ability to change, either needed some more Freedom or just needed to know
what Freedom was. Peace turns away from the mob and walks towards where*

Freedom was standing, Peace looks around and see's Beef standing behind a Mother and her son, with a look on his face that's showing how unrelaxed he is right now. Peace moves through the crowd of pedestrians, walks around the mother and son and puts his hand on Beef's shoulder, while Freedom stands right behind him watching everything move Beef makes. Beef makes eye contact with Peace and that's when Beef started to feel like there was no one around, except for him, Peace and Freedom. Jealousy looks over to where beef is and notices that Peace and Freedom has Beef, backed up into a corner. Jealousy tries to take a step away from War, towards Beef but Revenge steps in front of him and blocks his path. Now Jealousy, Envy and Hate are being faced off in a violent situation with Revenge, Penalty, Vengeance, Discipline and Justice and they all are having a serious verbal altercation. That looks and sounds like if Jealousy, Envy or hate to make the wrong move then the situation just might get physical, leaving a few casualties.

Revenge*:* Am I the only one here, really tired of Jealousy right now and these two cowards standing next to him, causing all this hate. Jealousy you and this two non-courage having, timid acting fools need to leave, before things get really difficult for all of you.

Jealousy: Looks who's talking, we'll if anybody should know you should Revenge and how this lifestyle has benefited us all, you see Revenge the only difference between me and you, is that I keep Envy and Hate alive. While you need someone to give out penalties and someone else to inflict punishment.

Revenge: Jealousy you've killed more peoples self-confidence than death and you've destroyed more relationships than divorce and injured more people than weapons, Jealousy your possessive insecurity is built on nothing but fear, you coward.

Envy: Revenge you are talking, when everybody knows that your day job, is only to punish people by your laws and rules you don't own. And to make things worse, you do it out of pure bitterness and resentment, through what only you consider as retaliation.

Hate: Revenge Hold up, you've not only retaliated for satisfaction but the desire and will that pushes you, was always initiated from corruption and animosity, based on the way you live with your man, whose name just so happens to be Jealousy.

Vengeance: You all talk a good one, but what I know for sure is that neither Jealousy, Envy or Hate belongs in this world. You all are like a deadly infectious disease, that nobody wants and definitely don't need.

Envy: Your killing me with the infectious disease theory Vengeance, you think just because your title is recorded in religious bible scriptures, that what you do will never get judged in court, or in front of a grand jury, or in the street. You are a fool and Vengeance is not yours, its mines.

Vengeance: Listen up Envy, you are the true definition of a follower, who's not even smart enough to follow people who's still useful after the harm and injuries has been done. Instead you follow backstabbers like Jealousy and Hate. Who really envy you, because at least you live with a desire to have, as far as Jealousy he lives with a feeling of vulnerability and Hate was born into being plain old prejudice.

Penalty: We'll isn't that the God honest truth and Envy you got the audacity, to get Jealous of other people's possessions and then turn around and Hate them, when they achieve greatness in their profession and reach their dreams and goals.

Jealousy: We all know how what Vengeance is really about, tell me who you ever imposed punishment on in a proper violation, when penalties were involved and If anything, you suffer the most from abiding by other people's Laws and Rules, which is definitely not yours. And that right there my friend is a person who lacks courage.

Hate: That's right and how do you enforce Vengeance, when you obey others and your influenced by what Hate does for a living. Plus, when there's no opportunity and no desire for you to perform your infamous duties, you become and start feeling just like the me, a certified hater.

Vengeance: Spoken like a true hater but it's sad when all that runs through your blood is Jealousy and Envy, which means if they run through your blood, that makes you their son so, which one of them Fathered you Jealousy or Hate.

War: And with that being said, Jealousy with your lack of self-confidence I don't understand how you could connect with anybody. I also believe the reason you are the way you are is because your self-image of wanting to feel special is poor. And Envy you have no qualities, your only reason for living is to acquire and obtain other people possessions, things you can't have. Which tells me that those female emotions you deal with, will never allow you to achieve. And last but not least we have Hate, who's emotional intense feelings derive from disliking people you know and don't know. That's someone who's active interactions on a daily basis is distasteful, hostile and resentful. Meaning you wake up every day, with a heart filled with animosity, so let me ask all three of you a question, why are you all still alive.

WAR

A Letter From Peace

On the block of confusion between trouble street and problem ave. The "Lives Matter" mob of individuals standing in the street shoulder to shoulder, with their arms interlocked now have the whole block surrounded. The scene looks and sounds like a crowd at a concert with no music playing and while the back and forth verbal altercation between Vengeance and Jealousy continues, War decides to check up on Peace. So, he leaves the altercation that's still taken place in the middle of the street and walks over to where Peace, Freedom and Beef are. War walks over by Peace and stands directly in front of Beef. War looks at Peace and Freedom and then back at Beef.

War looks back at Beef, who is standing there with his back against the wall, distraught and emotionally disturbed. Beef is nothing but confused right now at how and why Peace, Freedom and War are running together. But what Beef didn't realize is that without War there would be no Peace and without Peace there would be no Freedom and that's what made War want to put bring all this havoc and mayhem to an end. In the middle of the street Vengeance and Jealousy are still in a back and forth dispute as Peace steps in front of War, who's standing directly in front of Beef.

Peace looks back at Freedom and waits for the signal, Freedom nods his head up and down signaling that now is the time, Peace looks back at the mob of individuals standing side by side with their arms still interlocked. Peace then looks at Vengeance, Penalty and Revenge before turning back around and looking at Beef. Peace raises his arm and slowly reaches into his back pocket. Then all a sudden the sound of a gunshot goes off; the sound was so loud it echoes through the block of confusion between trouble street and problem ave.

"The sound of the gunshot made War duck down while covering his ears"

While the "Lives Matter" mob of individuals quickly release their interlocked arms and start ducking and running trying to take cover from the unknown active shooter. While Vengeance, Penalty, Revenge, Jealousy, Envy and Hate all separate from each other while ducking down as well, they disperse in different directions, also trying to take cover and get away from the unknown active shooter. Then right behind the first gunshot only seconds apart was another, this time the sound was even louder than the first. Now once a few feet away from the where he was standing,

War lifts his head up and notices that Peace and Freedom are still standing. War looks around but he doesn't see Beef, still ducking low War cautiously and slowly walks back over to where Peace and Freedom are. War raises up and can see Beef laying on the ground, with two bullet holes in his chest, Blood is soaking up his shirt and his eyes are wide open, War shakes his head side to side while feeling unfortunate for Beef, But War was confused, because when he looked at Peace, he didn't have a gun in either hand. War then looked at Freedom and he didn't have a gun in his hand either. This just didn't make since, because the last thing War cold remember was seeing Peace, reach into his back pocket and the only ones around was Peace and Freedom.

War places his hand on Peace shoulder, Peace looks war in the face with a look of satisfaction. Like what just happened happen for a real reason, then Freedom smiles and walks over and stands on the other side of War. Freedom raises his arm and points in the direction where Pain and Harm is slowly walking away calm, they both have a gun in each hand, as they both leave the scene of the crime, where Pain and Harm just killed Beef.

WAR

A Letter From Peace

*Guns have a **Mind** of their own*
*It's the shooters, who's not **Thinking**-*

*Pulling no **Conscious** index fingers*
On stupid triggers, that's brainless-

Leaving dummy bullets, to do all the teaching

WAR

A Letter From Peace

As police and ambulance sirens can be heard, War, Peace and Freedom rush to make their way away, from where Beef is lying on the ground dead, Freedom leads the way as Peace and War follows. Once far away from the crime scene and the police sirens and ambulances can't be heard as loud. War stops and grabs Peace by the arm, Peace stops surprisingly, Freedom then realizes War and Peace had stopped behind him. So, he turns around and walks a few feet back to where War and Peace are standing.

War: Peace you know what keeps bothering me and what I really can't get out of my head and believe me, it's definitely not seeing Beef, with two gunshot wounds in his body or even knowing that Beef was just killed. What I need to know is, what the hell were you reaching for in your back pocket, you carry a gun now Peace.

Freedom: Now that's funny, Peace carrying a gun that was invented to takes lives, when all of Peace life, he's forever since I can remember been about saving them.

War: I'm just saying, back there you not only had the look, you was about to do something to Beef, if not kill him and then you make sudden movements like a killer. Like reaching in your back pocket, while standing in front of your enemy. We'll if you ask me, if that don't make the person standing in front of you nervous and want to shoot first then what will.

Freedom: Just tell him, no as a matter of fact show him Peace.

War: Show me what.

Peace: War, what I was reaching for was a letter like the one I gave you, but the difference is this letter was written especially for Beef, handed directly to me by members of the "Lives Matter" movement with all intentions, of either changing Beef's life or ending it. I tried to get it to him, before Pain and Harm took his life away as you can see.

War: So, you mean to tell me you was reaching in your back pocket, in front of Beef someone who is known for the continuing of people's grudges and resentments, that's known for getting people shot and killed, your enemy and just to hand him a letter.

Peace: This wasn't just any letter; this was a letter of substance, a letter by a movement who's intention was to help change Beef and the world.

War: We'll if you ask me, there's no letter in this world worth me putting myself in a position, to get shot or killed.

Peace: Listen, Beef had Pain and Harm in his heart towards a lot of innocent and good people, people who wanted Freedom and just wanted to raise their family in Peace.

Peace: A life without having to look over their shoulders whenever they went to the grocery store, a life where they were going to be treated the same as their neighbor, whether or not if they are from different races. A life where job qualifications doesn't depend on who has a political connection, but who is the best man or woman for the job, a life where children can sit on a school bus and not get bullied, because the color of their skin, or the size of their waste or if their gender doesn't match their behavior.

Peace: So, the movement reached out to me and I got in touch with Freedom. I needed Freedom there because Freedom represents power, of not being mentally or physically imprisoned. And after I read the letter, I figured out that Freedom was the key to helping Beef become from being enslaved, from Pain and Harm, prejudice and mental imprisonment. Take a look at his killers Pain and Harm for instance, they did it because they were sick and tired of Beef waking up everyday thinking about his enemies and how he could end things with the help of Violence, who always escalated the situations when Beef was around.

Peace: Beef was the reason Jealousy, Envy and Hate was even born, Beef was also the reason so many grudges, arguments and fights never got resolved without someone getting shot, stabbed, jumped or placed on death row.

Peace: Beef was always acting like the boss towards Pain and Harm and they felt like they were working for Beef and whenever Beef was in the presence of a any altercation, it was followed by Pain and whenever Beef showed up with Jealousy, Envy and Hate on his mind, it was followed by Harm.

War: We'll I don't know about you Freedom and no disrespect to you Revenge, Penalty, Discipline or Justice, but I need to read that letter or have that letter read to me a.s.a.p.

Peace steps away from War and walks over to the store front, he turns around and leans his back up against the wall, Peace looks at Freedom who is now leaning up against a car hood, with his hands inside his pocket. While War stands a few feet away from them both, with his arms crossed anciently waiting to hear what this letter to Beef, from the "Lives Matter" movement is all about. Peace reaches into his ack pocket and takes out the letter, he unfolds the letter, holds it up away from his chest and starts reading.

The Letter...

To Beef
From The "Lives Matter" Movement

As we all sit here non-segregated wearing black t-shirts with "Lives Matter" written on it, we all think about how and why we follow in the shadows and uphold the "Black lives Matter" movement, against violence and racism. Not just towards black people, but towards all races around the world and one thing we've learned, is that Violence has a beginning and an end. And that beginning comes from a place, where a group of individuals or just two can interact with one another and disagree in the end with intentions to harm, or even kill each other from something as simple as a Beef.

(Letter Cont'd)

A Beef that could of started days, months or even years ago, this happens to often and will continue until we figure out, why people have problems so much with their own race or a different race and why they just can't seem to figure out how to disarm the violent anger, when involved in an altercation triggered by Retribution, Vengeance and Revenge, which would have never started, if the individuals would have just squashed the Beef.

We realize that there's many lives taken on the street and justice is the main focus, but we also realized that the aftermath to justice, is basically how a lot of innocent people get killed, how a lot of family members get harmed and a lot of children don't get to see their next birthday, when the Beef continues. This brings us back to you Beef and what part you play and what we think, we should do about it. We feel that you have been the heart of the intense abuse and hate, that escalates into War between the divisions of humankind to many times, Beef you are the seed that grows into stopping so many innocent children and adults from living free.

We feel that you are definitely in the way, for races wanting to carry on a productive and worry free life, simply because you continue on having generation after generation, past and present, wake up every day or go to sleep every night, with violent grudges and hostile thoughts of killing their enemy or harming their family or a family member, because the Beef will never settle. Therefore, we the "Lives Matter" movement and every organization that stands for Freedom, Justice and Equality revoke your pass on the block of confusion, between trouble street and problem avenue and all over the rest of the world. Beef you are no longer needed

With No Due Respect...

The "Lives Matter" Movement

WAR

A Letter From Peace

"*Violence is a violent behavior that physically involves force,*

with all intentions to hurt, damage or even kill its opponent.

Violence was built from the strength of people's emotions,

followed by the worlds unpleasant or destructive nature.

Violence is also intentional threats, targeted to attempt

or actually inflict person to person harm"

WAR

A Letter From Peace

*Violence was never **The Key***

*It's just another door, **That Lets You Enter** another room-*

*That houses more and **More Violence**.*

WAR

A Letter From Peace

The End...